AXEL & BEAST

TROPICAL TANGLE

ADRIAN C. BOTT ART BY ANDY ISAAC

Kane Miller
A DIVISION OF EDC PUBLISHING

First American Edition 2017
Kane Miller, A Division of EDC Publishing

Text Copyright © Adrian C Bott 2017
Illustration Copyright © Andy Isaac 2017
First published in Australia by Hardie Grant Egmont 2017

For information contact:
Kane Miller, A Division of EDC Publishing
P.O. Box 470663
Tulsa, OK 74147-0663
www.kanemiller.com
www.edcpub.com
www.usbornebooksandmore.com

Library of Congress Control Number: 2016955653

Printed and bound in the United States of America
1 2 3 4 5 6 7 8 9 10

ISBN: 978-1-61067-635-9

CHAPTER 1

The hot sun beat down on Junk City,
casting jagged shadows over a junkyard that
stretched as far as the eye could see. Light
glinted off twisted, windowless cars and
lit up the once-dark insides of abandoned
refrigerators. With the heat came the smell:
an overpowering mix of sludgy oil, rusting
metal and hot rubber, **pungent as an
android's armpit.**

In the middle of the yard, the junk had been arranged into walls. They formed a crude maze, which Axel and BEAST were halfway through.

Axel Brayburn couldn't feel the heat, but he was sweating anyway. From inside the air-conditioned cockpit of BEAST, his shape-shifting robot companion and best friend, Axel looked out over the heaps of junk.

"Nearly there, BEAST," he said. "We just need to sneak past the **patrol droid** and fit this **replacement power core** into the reactor at the heart of the maze. **Then the city will be saved!**"

BEAST looked at the object he was clutching in his right hand.

"BUT THIS IS NOT A REPLACEMENT POWER CORE, AXEL," he said.

Axel **rolled** his eyes.

"BEAST, would you just –"

"IT IS A BROKEN TOASTER."

Axel took a deep breath. "We've been over this."

"BEAST IS CONFUSED."

"I know it's a toaster. Just like the reactor is an old **ice cream truck,** and the patrol droid is Rusty Rosie in her **BULLDOZER.** But I need you to play along, okay?"

"SO THE CITY IS IN NO DANGER?"

"There isn't even a city near here!" Axel **groaned.** "This is a training exercise, remember? We're ***pretending*** there's an emergency, so we can practice dealing with them!"

It had been an interesting few weeks since BEAST had crashed into Axel's life. BEAST had originally been made as a suit of robot armor for another boy to wear – a spoiled, mean boy called Gus Grabbem Junior. Gus's father was the head of Grabbem Industries, the **greediest** corporation on the planet. Grabbem had wanted BEAST to rip the natural world apart so that they could get to the resources they wanted: oil, rare metals, gems and even buried nuclear fuel. But BEAST had had other ideas.

Now BEAST and Axel worked together to stop Grabbem's schemes whenever they could. An insider at Grabbem, Agent Omega, tipped them off to whatever new Grabbem plans were about to be unleashed.

At first Axel and BEAST had spent their time between missions hidden away in their **secret lair,** so that Grabbem wouldn't find them. However, the problem with hiding was that you never saw any **action,** which meant you never got to **learn.** After they'd run into danger on a mission to the Antarctic, Axel and his mother, Nedra, agreed some sort of regular training was needed.

So today they were in **JUNK CITY,** the junkyard that belonged to their friend Rusty Rosie. This "mission" had been her idea. She'd spent days building a maze out of scrap metal so that Axel and BEAST would have a real challenge. Now she was driving around in that same maze, playing the **bad guy,** hunting them down.

"Where are you creeps hiding?" her voice rang out. **"You going to come quietly or are you going to make me blast you out of there?"**

"She's right around the corner," Axel whispered.

He carefully steered BEAST back the way they'd come, moving as quietly as he could.

BEAST's big robot feet left footprint craters in the mud behind them.

Axel wondered if he should shift BEAST's form. BEAST could store five **apps** at a time, and each app let him change to a different shape with new abilities. The only problem was that each form had weaknesses as well as strengths.

He checked the current app list. **BOOSTA** was a **hot rod** form, superfast on land but really light on armor. **B-ZERK,** on the other hand, was a heavily armored **juggernaut** that moved slowly but had thick armor and a powerful cannon. Either might help ... or they might just make things harder. *Better wait and see*, he thought.

They were still making their way along the path between the piled-up junk walls when Axel spotted something that might be a shortcut. "See that gap in the wall, BEAST? Can you fit through?"

"HIGH PROBABILITY OF SUCCESS."

"Good enough. Let's take it."

They crawled through the gap and along a tunnel. Axel was sure it led straight to the maze's heart. Sure enough, through the opening up ahead he saw the pale-blue paint of the ice cream truck – their **mission objective.**

He scrambled out – and that was when the tower of cars came **crashing** down on them. Behind it was Rosie, grinning madly behind the wheel of her bulldozer. **"I KNEW IT! Had to take the shortcut didn't you? You fell right into my trap!"**

BEAST lay sprawled on his back, half-buried in wrecked cars. Axel stared up at the sky through BEAST's eyes.

"DOES THIS MEAN THE CITY IS DOOMED?" BEAST asked sadly.

"I'm not giving up as easily as that," Axel said through clenched teeth. There was still a chance to save the city, if he was brave enough to take it.

He shoved BEAST's canopy, trying to open it. It was stuck. He thumped it in frustration.

"Oh, come on – open, you **useless thing!**"

The canopy **popped** open. Axel leapt out of BEAST, grabbed the toaster out of his fat robotic hand and sprinted to the ice cream truck. A swift **SLAM DUNK** through the window and it was home.

"**Ah, nuts,**" said Rosie, twisting her cap around. "Well done, kid. You win."

"Yeah, but only just," laughed Axel. "That was hard!"

"You think so? I was going easy on you with the dozer," Rosie **grunted,** as she began to use the bulldozer to lift the cars off BEAST. "Next time I'll use the army surplus tank. That'll really **light** this place up."

BEAST struggled to his feet. He turned his head to the left and the right as if he wanted to make sure everything still worked. His eyes were small and sad.

"You okay, BEAST?" Axel asked.

"MY SYSTEMS ARE **FUNCTIONAL,**" BEAST said, and **stomped** off.

Axel watched him go. BEAST got a bit funny with games sometimes. *Maybe he's still learning how to have fun,* thought Axel, and shrugged. *He'll get used to it.*

Later, as Axel sat around the table with Rosie and his mother in Rosie's customized trailer home, there was a soft knock at the door.

They all fell silent and looked at one another. BEAST still hadn't come inside after their practice battle, but he was far too large to knock softly.

"Nobody's supposed to know we're here," Axel said.

"Wasn't expecting customers," Rosie said. "Yard's closed today, anyhow."

"It could be Grabbem," whispered Nedra.

Rosie stood up. "Sit tight. I'll deal with this. If any **bad business** goes down, **smash through** the back window and get out of here that way."

Axel's palms itched. He wished he had some way to send a message to BEAST and warn him.

Rosie opened the door a crack.

Outside was a tall, dark man in a heavy coat and mirrored glasses. The badge on his coat showed a fist with a *G* inside. The Grabbem symbol. Beneath it were the words: **MAXIMUM SECURITY**.

"Yeah?" said Rosie.

"I'm looking for Axel," said the man.

CHAPTER 2

Axel knew that strange, hoarse voice. He'd heard it before, but never in person.

The man glanced nervously over his shoulder. "Rosie, it's me. Let me in. I've got something for Axel."

"Agent Omega!" Axel yelled. "Is it you?"

Agent Omega winced. "Not so loud. You never know who might be listening."

Rosie pulled him into the trailer. He glanced around, as if checking for exits. He had the nervous, worried look of a **hunted animal.**

"Where's BEAST?" he asked.

Axel pointed downward. "He's in his cave in GOPHER mode. Wanted to be by himself. He gets like that sometimes."

Agent Omega relaxed a little. He squeezed in next to Nedra, who poured him some super-strong coffee. She tried to take his coat, but he insisted on keeping it on, despite the hot day.

There was an awkward silence. He cleared his throat. "Apologies for coming in person."

"Nonsense. It's lovely to meet you at last," Nedra said.

"It seemed the safest way to deliver this." He passed Axel a shiny black case about the size of a large envelope.

Inside the case was something that looked like a pair of sunglasses, formed in a single wraparound piece. The lenses were jet-black. Axel could just make out tiny circuits embedded in the material.

"It's a **smart visor,**" Omega explained. "Put it on. It'll fit over your glasses – I designed it to."

"You made this? **For me?**" Axel asked, amazed.

"Oh, yes. And I used Grabbem equipment to do it. I like fighting them with their own weapons."

The smart visor was so light it was like wearing nothing. At first it seemed to do nothing, too. Axel could see just like normal.

He didn't want to be ungrateful so he said, "It's very cool. Thanks."

"It responds to your thoughts," Agent

Omega explained. "Think about seeing through things, and you'll be able to."

X-ray, thought Axel.

Suddenly he was looking at a **human skull with veiny eyeballs.** It **gnashed** its jaws at him.

"Arrr!" he yelled, and nearly jumped out the window in horror. The view swiftly changed back to Agent Omega's worried face.

"You might want to take it easy with that one," Omega said, "but it should come in handy for seeing through walls. You can also use the visor to scan for **heat signatures.** Oh, and it'll show you what keys to press to **hack** any Grabbem terminal."

"That's amazing!"

"All that stuff – isn't that what BEAST does?" asked Nedra.

"Same technology," said Agent Omega.

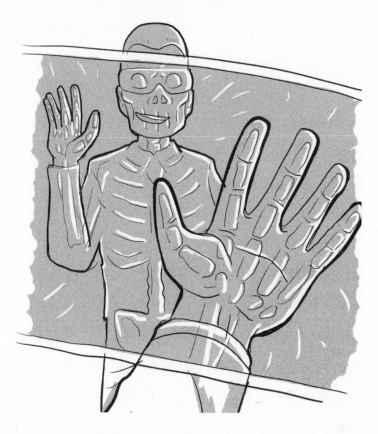

"But with the smart visor, Axel will be able to do it by himself."

"Sweet!" said Axel. He held up his hand and looked at the finger bones. "Whoa. Skeleton hand. Creepy."

Agent Omega frowned. "Let's get down to business. I'm not just here to hand out presents. I've got an assignment for you." He produced a slim silver laptop from under his coat.

"I'll go fetch BEAST," said Axel.

"There's no time. Brief him yourself after I've gone."

Agent Omega turned the laptop so that Axel could see. The screen showed a green island surrounded by **sparkling** blue water.

"This is Stormhaven Island. It's in the middle of the Pacific Ocean. Gus Grabbem Senior owns it, as well as the ocean around it for miles. He's built a house there."

Axel looked longingly at the wide sandy beaches and palm trees. His arch rival, **Gus Grabbem Junior,** got to sun himself on those beaches – spoiled brat that he was, he probably didn't even appreciate it. But by the look on Nedra's face, she wished she could go there, too. Her travel suitcases had been at the top of the closet for a long time.

"That house is a cover for some kind of **secret base**," Agent Omega went on. "Grabbem are building something there – their biggest project in years. They call it the **Plunderer.**"

Axel's mind raced as he tried to think what the Plunderer might be. A warship? A tank? It could be a giant **two-headed cyborg battle hamster** for all he knew.

"There's more. I've decoded some Grabbem emails," said Agent Omega, "and it seems they're planning on detonating a **bomb** out there. **An atomic bomb.**"

"Whoa," said Rosie.

Nedra looked sick. "How *could* they?"

"Why would they do that?" asked Axel.

"It's meant to power the Plunderer somehow. Don't ask me how – it's a mystery to me. But there's rich and varied **marine wildlife** in that part of the ocean, and an island atoll nearby," Omega said. "The damage from an atomic bomb would be ... yuck. I don't even want to think about it."

Axel nodded. "So what's the plan?"

"Get inside that base and stop the launch of the Plunderer. You need to be extra stealthy on this one, though. If that means going solo so you can get into places BEAST can't go, then do it."

Axel fingered the visor. "Okay. I understand. What about apps?"

Agent Omega slid a USB drive across the table. "You'll need **BLACKBAT,** which BEAST already has. There are four new apps on the USB for you." He counted them on his fingers. **"MANTA** is a new **underwater** form that's sneaky and quick, to replace **SHARKOS** for this mission. **OCTO** is clearly **octopus mode:** eight strong tentacles for lifting and moving things. **HARPY** is a **flying heavy lifter,** with two claw grabbers." He paused. "And then there's **ORBITA. Just in case."**

"What's that one for?"

"I don't expect you'll need it. It's just that ... well, we don't know what the Plunderer even is or where it operates, so I thought you'd better be prepared for *any* environment ..." His voice trailed off.

"Well?" Nedra demanded.

Agent Omega took his glasses off. Axel was a little startled to see that he had ordinary human eyes under there. Omega was so tech-minded, Axel had wondered if he might be a cyborg.

"ORBITA is a zero-gravity form," said Omega. **"For operations in space."**

CHAPTER 3

At the Grabbem mansion, Gus Grabbem Junior **kicked** open the double doors to the dining room. His mother and father were already seated at opposite ends of the enormous table, with a wall of fresh toast between them.

The butler, Lucius, watched steadily as Gus **swaggered** in and flung himself onto a chair.

"Good morning, sir," Lucius said.

"Morning, **goat breath**," said Gus.

Lucius was an accomplished actor and had once been part of a posh British theater company. He was very good at hiding his real feelings. "Would you care for some breakfast?" he asked.

"Sure, **flunky.** Get me some toast. And use those tongs. I don't want your fingers all over it."

Inside his mind, Lucius was imagining how much he would enjoy smashing Gus's electric guitar over his head. On the outside, however, he was perfectly calm. Not even a **nostril hair** quivered as he dished up the food.

Gus bit, chewed and **spat** a wad out onto his plate. "This toast's cold."

"Please don't be a fussy Gussie," said his mother, with a hand to her head. "You'll give

Mommy a headache, and you don't want to do that. Not today."

"What's so special about today?" Gus put his feet up on the table.

"Today's the day we launch the Plunderer," grunted Gus's father from behind his newspaper. "We're heading out to the island house in an hour. You've not forgotten your special job, have you?"

"Oh, yeah. I get to press the **big red button!**"

"That's right," grinned Gus Senior. "My little boy gets to trigger his first atomic blast!" He dabbed a sentimental tear from his eye.

Just then, a man in a captain's uniform stepped into the room. He **bulged** in all sorts of places, like a badly baked **loaf of bread** that was made of muscle. He took off his hat. His head was shaved. Scars and tattoos were in the middle of a turf war across his skin.

"Reporting for duty, sir."

Gus Grabbem Senior stood up, folded his paper away and gave the man a friendly **whack** on the shoulder. He didn't budge.

"Fenton! Good to see you, skipper. Take a seat."

"Prefer to stand, sir," said the man. "I'm not one for comfort."

Gus Junior looked the man up and down. Something was happening in Gus Junior's brain that didn't usually happen, and he didn't like it. He knew, in the deep-down way that you know certain true things, that this stranger wouldn't be as easy to push around as the rest of the Grabbem staff. So he did what he always did. He turned his fear into rudeness.

"Hey, Dad. Who's the **Frankenstein?**"

Lucius, who was tidying up the breakfast dishes, let out the tiniest of excited squeaks. Inside, he was thinking: *Please, oh please, let the* **ghastly** *little brat push this hard nut too far, and get the spanking he so richly deserves!*

"This is Captain Fenton," said Gus Senior. "He'll be in charge of the Plunderer."

"Thirty years' naval experience, as both man and boy," said Fenton, his chest swelling with what might have been pride.

Gus Junior gave a scornful sniff. **"Big deal.** I could steer the Plunderer myself if I had to."

Fenton slowly went and stood behind Gus's chair. He leaned in close to Gus's ear and whispered: "Maybe you could. But the sea can be a frightening place, young fella.

Some real nasty characters turn up on board ships. And the thing is, once you've put to sea, you can't just hop off again if you decide you don't like it. So it's best to put a man like me in charge. I'm not trying to scare you. Just want you to be realistic."

Gus swallowed. "I can look after myself."

Fenton placed his hand, heavy as a shovel, on Gus's shoulder. He **squeezed**, hard. It hurt.

Gus tried not to wince, but the pain showed on his face.

"Just do as you're told, sunshine, and we'll get along famously," breathed Fenton. He gave Gus's shoulder a final pat and turned back to Gus Senior. "Care to meet the first mate, sir?"

"Send him in! Let's see what my money is paying for."

Gus Junior was already uncomfortable. When he saw the **metal horror** that came stalking into the room, he became **downright scared.** It was like a **robot pirate**, with multiple arms and a chrome skull for a face.

"Presenting **U-WOT-M8**," said Fenton. "Not just a reliable first mate, but a cracking chief of security, too. Armed with the *deadliest* weapons, and clever enough to know when to use them. **Knows when to stun and when to kill.** Its senses are so fine, they even work on the **pheromone** level."

"What does that mean?" snapped Gus Junior.

"He can **smell** fear," Fenton whispered down to Gus Junior, as he requested a salute from the robot pirate.

Gus Senior put his hands on his hips and

looked up approvingly at the **square-jawed** metal face. "You can tell this thing's your baby, Fenton. He looks like you!"

U-WOT-M8 had tiny little red eyes. Just for a second, they *glowed.*

Fenton smiled.

CHAPTER 4

It was long after nightfall, and BEAST was flying through the sky in BLACKBAT form. His arms had **transformed** to two wide, flat wings. Tall antenna ears listened out for enemy signals.

With its full **stealth** powers activated, BLACKBAT's metal skin changed to match its environment. This meant it was completely invisible against the night sky. Axel had to make sure he steered well clear of planes because a pilot could easily crash into him.

Axel loved flying over cities in BLACKBAT, looking down on all the buildings filled with people who didn't even know he was there. *I'm a silent guardian,* he thought, *flying over the rooftops at night. I wonder if this is what it's like to be Santa Claus.*

But they had left the last of the cities behind long ago, and now they were flying over miles and miles of open sea. There were still **wonderful** things to see here: the huge flukes of a whale's tail, the lights of small and large ships making long ocean journeys, and even an island atoll, which Axel had learned was the coral-encrusted remains of an extinct, sunken **volcano.** But mostly it was just ocean, which meant Axel had plenty of time to think.

"What do you think this Plunderer might be, BEAST?"

"BEAST DOES NOT KNOW," said BEAST. "I AM SORRY, AXEL. BEAST IS **USELESS** SOMETIMES."

"Don't worry about it." Axel decided not to bother discussing the Plunderer with BEAST anymore. BEAST had been a bit **moody** lately, for some reason.

But in his private thoughts, Axel kept turning it over and over, like a **scab** you can't help picking at. *Maybe the Plunderer is a laser satellite.* **Or a flying saucer.** *Or a new battle suit for Gus Grabbem Junior, to replace BEAST. But how could any of those be powered by an atomic bomb?*

"DESTINATION AHEAD," BEAST announced.

Stormhaven Island appeared before them

in the moonlight, rising out of the ocean like the shell of a **monstrous crab.** Thick jungle covered the island's surface, except for the long, sloped sandy beaches and the part where a small mountain broke up through the dark greenery.

Axel spotted a white structure near one stretch of beach. *That's the Grabbem house. The rest of the base is underneath, hidden from sight.*

He slowed down their airspeed and came closer to sea level. BLACKBAT was silent, but there were other ways to give yourself away to an alert enemy – an unexpected *gust* of wind was one of them.

"Gently does it," he said. "Let's get a good look at that house ..."

WHOOSH!

The next second, Axel was wrenching

BLACKBAT around in the air, steering it sharply away from ... **what?** Something had flashed up in front of him. Something red against the darkness.

He'd acted on pure reflex. Now his heart was pounding. He felt he'd just avoided some kind of terrible disaster, but he didn't even know why. He kept BLACKBAT hovering above the water, the length of a football field or two away from the house, and checked the readouts.

"BEAST, can you detect anything out there? Anything hidden?"

"SCANNING," BEAST replied.

BLACKBAT's ear-antennae **wiggled** back and forth as the sophisticated instruments went to work.

It didn't take the robot long to find what he'd been looking for. He adjusted Axel's view screen so that he could see them, too.

Ghostly transparent shapes appeared on the screen, hovering silently in the air. They were like **metallic insects** with rotors instead of wings. They hung over the whole island like a swarm of sand flies, and they shone dim red beams of laser light between themselves, forming a grid around the house. No doubt anything that broke one of those beams would trigger an alarm … or worse.

"Sentry drones," Axel said with a **shudder.** "We nearly ran right into them."

"I AM SORRY, AXEL," said BEAST. "I SHOULD HAVE DETECTED THEM SOONER."

"Don't sweat it. We're both going to have to up our game for this one, huh. Come on. Let's see if there's a gap in those beams somewhere."

BLACKBAT swept through the air, graceful and invisible, while the drones **hummed** and **flickered** their sinister beams. Axel soon realized there wasn't a single spot where you could fit anything bigger than a basketball through the grid.

Axel racked his brains to think of a way in. Those drones were screening off the house from the air. Okay, that meant they couldn't fly in. But what about under the ocean surface? Were there drones there, too?

"Change of plan, BEAST. Shift to MANTA form!"

BEAST morphed and changed in midair. His body became broad and flat. A long, jointed tail made from metal plates extended from his back.

They plowed into the dark water. Axel had expected a splash, but there was nothing but the softest of **slopping** sounds, like an otter slipping into a stream.

"Wow. That was smooth."

MANTA felt completely different to SHARKOS. Driving SHARKOS was like being at the wheel of a powerful speedboat that **tore** through the water with power and attitude. But MANTA just slipped through the water like a blade through silk, meeting no resistance at all. MANTA seemed so stealthy that not even the sea noticed it passing through.

Axel cautiously circled the entire island, scanning for enemies the whole time. Fish darted away from them as they approached. Coral **glistened** in the undersea moonlight.

"Looks like we're clear. No bad guys here. **Whoa, what's that?"**

Off the main beach, hidden deep under the waves, was a gigantic opening in the rocky island edge. Metal panels sealed it off.

"IT IS A DOOR," said BEAST.

"Yeah, but look at the size of it! It must lead straight into the Grabbem base. That means it's something to do with the Plunderer. It has to be!" Axel looked thoughtfully at his smart visor. "Too bad it doesn't have a terminal I could hack."

Lights flashed inside BEAST's cockpit. "IF WE TRANSMITTED THE CORRECT CODE, THE DOOR WOULD OPEN. I AM SORRY, AXEL. I DO NOT KNOW THE CODE."

"Well, we're not getting in that way. Let's head for the beach and then come up inside the drones' field. They're all facing outward, so they won't see us."

MANTA **slid** as silently as a shadow from the deeper waters toward the shallows. Axel held his breath as they drew closer to their goal. This was going to work. Once they were past that funny rock formation, BEAST could just wade out of the water in his regular form ...

That's no rock formation!

Axel quickly **braked,** jabbing MANTA's tail into the seabed like an emergency anchor.

MANTA jerked to a stop. Axel's head **whacked** against BEAST's safety padding.

They had stopped just in time. A many-legged shape heaved itself up from the sand right in front of them. Clouds of sand and sediment swirled up around it. Axel saw **massive pincers** the color of rusty iron, eyes like spotlights on long stalks, and a segmented body that was plated with **armor** as thick as a battleship.

Drones above the water, Axel thought, *and beneath, whatever this thing is. I should have known Grabbem would make this tricky.*

"Grabbem use **robot lobsters** as guards now?" he said.

"IT IS THE LOBSTRON 6.3. AN OLD MODEL," said BEAST, "BUT STILL EXTREMELY DANGEROUS."

The Lobstron glanced side to side through

the clouds of silt, looking for what had disturbed it. It seemed grumpy somehow. It **clashed its pincers,** as if it was trying to warn anything lurking out in the deep that it wasn't to be messed with.

"I don't think it's very bright," Axel whispered.

"THE LOBSTRON BRAIN IS ABOUT EQUAL TO A RABBIT," said BEAST.

Now the Lobstron was scuttling back and forth across its area of seabed, like a **crotchety** old castle guard who has been woken up and forced to do a patrol when all he really wants to do is sleep.

"It hasn't seen us," said Axel. "But it's bound to if we go any closer. Hold on. I've got an idea."

He brought MANTA down to the seabed and then kept going, driving its smooth, flat form into the soft sand, just like a flatfish camouflaging itself. Once MANTA was completely buried and he was sure they wouldn't be seen, he **whipped up** the tail and **waggled** it.

The Lobstron noticed. It squinted into the murk. Something was out there, but its aged eyes couldn't quite make it out. It scuttled down the sandy slope on its many metal legs, occasionally **snapping** its pincers menacingly.

A **wheezy, bubbly voice** came through BEAST's internal speakers: **"WHO GOES THERE?"**

No *wonder BEAST said it was dangerous,* Axel thought, as he waited in the heart-thumping dark. *Those pincers could **slice** a tank's gun barrel off.*

He heard a nerve-jangling **scraping**

noise as the Lobstron's legs scrabbled over the rocks and onto MANTA's back.

Then it stopped.

Right on top of them.

CHAPTER 5

The Lobstron squatted on top of BEAST, as he lay in the sand in his flat MANTA form. It looked around, **squinting** into the murky darkness.

Axel held his breath, hovering his hand over the control that moved MANTA's tail. He might be able to get in one solid hit before the Lobstron went on the attack. It wasn't much of a chance, but it was better than nothing.

He touched the control – and then he hesitated.

The sound of **grinding** metal was back. The Lobstron was moving again, stalking farther down into the deeper sea. It was still looking for the mysterious thing it had seen.

When the dreadful sound of the scraping legs had faded away completely, Axel breathed out all at once.

"Brain of a rabbit," he gasped. "Some rabbit."

"BEAST IS GLAD WE DID NOT HAVE TO FIGHT."

"Yeah. If you'd been in SHARKOS form, it would have been another story. Let's get out of here before it comes back."

In his regular robot form, BEAST began striding up out of the sea. Water ran off him and flowed away down the sand. A starfish was clinging to his bottom. Through the transparent canopy in his chest, Axel watched the water level go down and down.

There, at the top of the sandy rise, was the Grabbem mansion. Somewhere inside were the **secrets** of the Plunderer.

Spotlights shone down from towers all around the house. They were as bright as the lights at a soccer stadium, but they moved slowly back and forth.

Axel kept BEAST away from the lights, safe in the outer shadows where they wouldn't be seen. Once he'd come as close as he dared, he stopped. "That's as far as we can go together."

"BUT WE NEED TO GET INSIDE."

Axel sighed. **"No."**

"… BEAST DOES NOT UNDERSTAND. YOU HAVE ANOTHER PLAN?"

"*We* aren't going in there, BEAST. I am. **Alone.**"

"BUT AXEL AND BEAST ARE A **TEAM**."

Axel laughed. "Don't worry about me. I'll do fine on my own."

"FINE ON YOUR OWN?" echoed BEAST.

Axel tried again. "BEAST, this is a stealth mission, remember? I have to get inside without being seen. And you're a big robot. **A fantastic, awesome robot, yeah.** But definitely **a big one.** Do you understand what I'm saying?"

BEAST was silent.

"I'll be super careful. I promise."

"WHAT IS BEAST MEANT TO DO WITHOUT YOU?"

"Just hide. Stay away from any patrols. Don't get into **fights** with any strange robots or anything."

"OKAY," BEAST said, not sounding okay.

"I won't be gone long."

Axel punched the canopy release and went to open it. **It was stuck, yet again.** He **thumped** it until it opened, climbed out of BEAST and took a deep breath. The air out in the middle of the Pacific Ocean was cool and clean, and salty from the sea. It shook him awake, after having been **cooped up** inside BEAST for so long.

He put on the new visor that Agent Omega had given him.

Instantly he could see as clearly as day, even though it was night. Invisible features of the Grabbem house stood out as brightly as fireworks – secret pressure-pad traps, crisscrossing alarm beams, even some sort of snakelike thing lurking under the house's front lawn.

He relaxed a little. Now he didn't feel quite so much like a **hapless newbie** blundering into a deadly labyrinth. He felt like a trusted agent.

He turned to wave good-bye to BEAST. The robot was sitting in a huddle on the sand, **hugging** his knees.

Is he trying to disguise himself as a rock? Axel thought. *That's weird.*

Axel had never had any **secret agent training** – very few kids of his age ever get the chance, though some are lucky enough to – but he was a gamer through and through. He'd played enough **stealth** games to know the sort of thing he should be doing right now.

He went through the checklist in his mind:

Stay out of the light.

Use cover.

Plan ahead.

Move only when you have to, and always know where you're going next.

He ran barefoot across the sand, keeping to the dark areas between the moving spotlights. Halfway across, as the spotlights swung back, he **dived** behind a rock and waited for their blinding glare to pass. When he was in darkness once again he moved on.

He leapt over a **trip wire** that would have caught any normal human, but stood out in his vision like a **red-hot sparkler.** A quick dash over cold paving stones, and he was up to the front wall of the house. The wall was made from smooth marble blocks, no doubt costing a fortune.

This is amazing, he thought. He felt more alive than ever before. His blood seemed to sing with energy.

Where now? Could he just walk up to the front door and expect to get in? There didn't seem to be any guards here, neither human nor robot. **Best to make sure, though.** He tapped the smart visor and switched it to its most sensitive **heat-detection setting.**

There. Like human figures made from purple flame, the **heat signatures** of three people were clear in his view. They were in a room just inside the house, and they were sitting down. So they must be awake then, and alert.

Probably guards on night duty having a casual chat, Axel figured. *Chatting about what, though? The Plunderer, maybe?*

He had to know.

He just had to get inside this **island fortress** of a mansion somehow. He stayed completely still, letting his gaze rove over the front of the house. He looked at the hundreds of dark windows; none were open. There were no drainpipes to climb. The sheer marble walls offered no inviting ledges to pull himself up onto. If this had been a movie about a **kid secret agent,** he could have unscrewed an air vent and climbed inside it. But the only air vents he could see were on the roof, and only about six inches across.

Well, he thought, *there's always the front door.*

He looked carefully at the riveted metal door, which looked like it belonged on a **warship.** He narrowed his eyes as he noticed the little box alongside the door.

A keypad.

"What did Agent Omega say about the smart visor hacking Grabbem terminals?" he whispered to himself. "I hope keypads count ..."

He **sidled** over to the door. The keypad box glowed in the dark like a charging smartphone. He reached up to it and held his fingers out.

The visor **whirred** with wild colors for a full minute as it made its calculations. Then four of the keypad buttons lit up in order.

Axel tapped them quickly, his hands shaking.

A soft **click**, a *hiss* of pressurized air, and the door swung **open.**

I did it. I'm in ...

CHAPTER 6

Once, when Axel was a little boy, he'd visited a friend's house. They had played **hide-and-seek.** Axel's first hiding place – the cupboard under the stairs – had been way too obvious, and so he had been determined to do something special for the next one.

He had ended up wandering into a part of the house he hadn't ever seen before. It was where his friend's granny lived, but he hadn't known that at the time. He hid under the old woman's bed. He lay there among the dust bunnies and dropped tissues as the minutes ticked by. His friend's searching shouts became even more desperate.

Then his friend's granny came into the room and lay down on the bed for a rest. Axel lay **paralyzed** underneath her, hardly daring to breathe. He knew that if he tried to escape she would see him, and probably scream her head off.

He had felt **terrified,** and yet **thrilled** at the same time.

That long-ago moment came back to him now as he slipped through the metal door and into the hallway of the Grabbem mansion.

The hallway was long and wide and featureless, apart from a huge painting of Gus Grabbem Senior that hung at the end. The portrait scowled at Axel. He looked like a **toad in a business suit.** Axel watched his eyes to see if they moved, but they didn't.

From behind a nearby door came the sound of voices.

Axel crept up to the door, which was open a crack, and **peeked** in.

It was a security room, with dozens of screens on the wall. Two men and a woman sat around a table with their sleeves rolled up, drinking coffee. Grabbem guards.

"… we're going to get a raise, no question," said the one nearest the door.

"We won't get a raise. They'll just give us company credits or something, to spend on more Grabbem merchandise," the woman said. "Costs them less that way."

"But this is different," insisted the first guard. "And I'm going to tell you why it's different."

Wow, this is dynamite stuff, Axel thought wearily. *I don't know what I expected. These are just working people talking about work.*

"This here island is going to become **Grabbem Central,** because it's the Plunderer's base of operations," explained the guard. "That thing's going to **tear** through the ocean floor like a hog going after truffles, **raking up** all sorts of goodies. Gold, rare minerals, diamonds even! Anything gets in its way – coral reefs or whatever – it'll just **chew** right through them. I tell you, guys, we're in the right place!"

Axel's heart nearly **exploded** from excitement. *That explains the huge door we saw,* he thought. *The Plunderer is an underwater mining machine! Typical Grabbem – just ripping the world apart to get what they want. But how does the bomb fit in?*

"We aren't supposed to talk about the Plunderer," warned the third guard, who hadn't spoken yet.

"Ah, nuts to that," snapped the first. "We've kept quiet this long, and anyway, who's going to be listening? We're in the middle of the ocean!"

Axel mouthed a **"hello"** and waved at them through the wall, knowing they wouldn't see.

"Walls have ears, that's what they say," the third guard said.

A chair scraped. One of the guards had stood up. "Boys, I'm going to grab a shower," she said. "The boss gets here in less than an hour. Captain Fenton and his **scary first mate** will be joining us then, too. If I were you, I'd tidy this place up a bit before Fenton sees it. You know what he's like."

"Man, do I ever," said the first guard.

The female guard was coming toward the door.

Axel turned and ran. His bare feet made **no noise** on the thick carpets. As the door swung open behind him, Axel came up to the portrait of Gus Grabbem. With no other idea of what to do, he *dashed* around a corner to the left.

Ahead was another long, marble-walled corridor, much like the first. *You could get lost in here really easily,* Axel thought. Through glass doors along the corridor's length he saw the palatial rooms that lay beyond: a gym, a game room, some kind of luxury lounge.

He sprinted down to the corridor's end, turned the corner and found a spiral staircase. *Up or down?* He could hear voices from the floor below. *Better head up, then,* he thought, and sprinted up the stairs.

They led up and up, through echoing galleries and past halls filled with ugly statues, until the stairs ran out. Axel pushed through the door ahead of him and – to his surprise – suddenly found himself standing on the flat roof.

He paused to catch his breath. Nobody had seen him yet, and there was a superb view of the island from up here. The door hadn't shut behind him, so he still had a way back down. The situation could be **a lot worse.**

He craned his neck to look up and down the beach, trying to see if BEAST was still there – but the robot was nowhere to be seen. *Please be okay,* he thought. Then he sat down on the cool, rough roof surface and pondered his next move.

Being all alone up here reminded him of playing as a **sniper** in online battles. Maybe he could use the roof as a lookout point and spy on the Grabbems as they arrived. One of them might let something slip about where the bomb was.

He crept to the roof's edge, lay flat on his stomach, leaned over and focused on the beach.

He touched the smart visor. **MAGNIFY,** he thought.

The view zoomed in. He scanned back and forth. Perfect. All he had to do now was wait.

The next hour passed as slowly as a wet summer. Axel found himself wishing BEAST were there so that they could make up terrible **knock-knock** jokes together. That always made the time fly past.

A warm breeze blew as the sun came up. A bustle of movement began inside the house. The front courtyard filled with lined-up members of the household staff: guards, maids, butlers, cooks, all in dazzling white uniforms and looking nervous. One of them looked at his watch.

Axel spotted a gleaming white yacht on the horizon. A helicopter took off from the yacht's deck and flew toward the island. It passed through the drone defense grid, which **flickered red** as the chopper broke the beams. The chopper touched down in front of the house and people began to get out.

Out came Gus Grabbem Senior himself, then his wife, then his son. The staff all saluted stiffly. Gus Grabbem Junior made a rude sign at them, which was also – strictly speaking – a kind of salute.

Then came a man with muscular flesh **bulging** out of his uniform, like an overstuffed samosa. *Captain Fenton*, thought

Axel. Behind him trundled a **hideous robotic creature,** like something off one of Gus Junior's thrash metal album covers. Its head was a red-eyed silver skull, and six arms sprouted from its upper body.

The sight of it made Axel's flesh creep.

"Glad BEAST isn't here to see this," he whispered to himself. "'Scary first mate' is right."

The more he looked at it, the more **deep-down afraid** he felt. Sweat began to gather on his forehead. A drop fell and landed on the concrete far below.

The hideous six-armed robot suddenly jerked into life. Its metal skull tilted slowly up and looked right at Axel. The tiny red dots of its eyes widened into **hot-crimson lenses.**

Captain Fenton glanced at it. "What is it,

first mate? Something to report?"

"**Feeeeeaaaaarrrr,**" grated the robot.

"Come again?"

"**I. Can. Smell. *Feeeeeaaaaarrr.***"

Axel lay absolutely still, feeling **sick** with panic. There could be no doubt. The robot had smelled him, and now he was as good as **dead.**

Gus Grabbem Senior gave Fenton a sidelong glance. "What is wrong with your first mate? He's not blown a circuit, has he?"

"Must just be a bit oversensitive," Captain Fenton said. "Probably smells a monkey in the trees or something. I'll give him a tweak with the old screwdriver later on ..."

"**I SMELL FEAR!**" bellowed the robot.

It pushed past Fenton, knocking him aside ...

CHAPTER 7

Axel scrambled to his feet and away from the ledge. Without the slightest idea where he would run to, he began running along the flat roof.

He could hear Captain Fenton yelling below: "Stop right now, U-WOT-M8! There's nothing there! Get back, I tell you!" But the hulking robot wasn't listening. It had Axel's scent now and it was **on the hunt.**

Waving all six of its arms, it charged straight through the lined-up Grabbem staff. They screamed and ran to the left and right, **trampling** the flower beds and dropping whatever they carried. A silver tray piled with sandwiches fell with a **crash.**

The robot paused and looked up at the sheer wall of the house. Then it crouched, sprang and clamped itself to the outside of the house like an ugly metal spider. Two of its six arms ended in cutlass-like blades, and it crunched them deep into the stone to hold on.

Gus Grabbem winced. "That damage is coming out of your salary," he told Fenton.

Meanwhile, Axel was running. He looked over his shoulder and saw U-WOT-M8 heaving itself over the edge of the roof. The glowing red eyes **locked** on to him.

"BEAST, wherever you've gotten to, now would be a really good time to show up!" he panted.

This could be worse, he told himself. *Yes, I'm being chased by a hideous six-armed robot-assassin thing that probably wants to carve me up like a kebab, and no, I don't have any weapons, and BEAST is who knows where. But so far, the only thing that's seen me is the robot. All the humans down there think it's faulty. So I haven't blown my cover yet. I still might get out of this alive.*

Without warning, Axel ran out of roof.

There was nowhere left to run, just a sheer drop.

GULP!

Okay. It had just gotten worse.

U-WOT-M8 began to scrape its blades together as it approached, just like Axel's dad used to do when sharpening the knife before carving a roast.

Axel wobbled on the edge. There was no staircase or ladder down. There wasn't even a balcony he could lower himself onto. There was just the lawn at the back of the house, and the swimming pool with deck chairs set around it.

The pool was full. It was a chance, if he dared to take it. But he'd have to get a good run up to it, and that would mean …

He moved before **terror** could stop him. He ran back across the roof, right into the path of the oncoming robot. Metal arms unfolded like umbrella ribs, ready to **clasp** him close. The skull let out a **shriek of victory.**

Axel skidded to a stop, turned around and sprinted for the building's edge. Instead of slowing down, he sped up. He *launched* himself off, aiming for the pool, and all the terror burst out of him in one long, drawn-out scream as he fell.

"WHOAAAA!"

He tumbled through the air, not knowing if he would reach the water or shatter his bones on the ground.

The next second, the water's stinging fist **smashed** into him. He plunged down to the bottom, bubbles streaming from his nose and mouth.

I did it. I'm alive.

His whole body ached; the impact had hit him hard. But he forced himself to swim to the edge and pull himself out.

As he lay gasping beside the pool, he saw the robot **glaring** down at him from the top of the house.

"Yeah, follow me now if you can, you **ugly piece of junk,**" he muttered, as he pulled himself to his feet.

To his dismay, the robot latched two of its bladed arms on to the edge and then began to lower itself down, the arms telescoping out as it went. It abseiled like a spider all the way to the ground, then unhooked its arms and sucked them back to normal length.

"Oh, man!" Axel set off at a run once again. "Doesn't this thing ever give up?"

Beyond the lawns lay the untamed jungle that covered the rest of the island. Axel ran between the trunks of towering trees and felt **spongy** moss under his feet. Great bushy ferns brushed him as he shot past. Hopefully, all this thick vegetation would slow the oncoming robot down a little and give him time to think of a plan.

U-WOT-M8 powered after him, spinning its blades like some barbarian war chariot from ancient times. It reached the jungle and plunged in. Instead of swerving around the palm trees, it just *lashed* out with its bladed arms. The blades whipped through the thick trunks as if they were only mist. They fell with a *groan* and a *crash*, showing white, moist wood inside.

"HALT, INTRUDER," it rasped. **"YOU ARE NOT AUTHORIZED TO BE HERE. YOU MUST BE QUESTIONED."**

"I'm the pool boy!" Axel yelled.

"INCORRECT."

"Worth a try," gasped Axel. He bounded up the edge of a rocky slope. As he climbed farther, he realized it was the beginnings of the crumbling hill that rose up and out of the greenery. Maybe if he kept going, the ground would be too uneven for the robot to stand.

The horrible chase went on, with Axel reaching higher and higher ground and the seemingly unstoppable robot clambering after him. Soon he found he was right at the top of the rocky outcrop, on a ledge that jutted out over the jungle, with the robot closing in.

"DO NOT MOVE," warned the robot.

Axel doubled over, spluttering, hoping the robot would think he was finished. As his hands dangled near the ground, he quickly snatched up a fist-sized lump of rock. One good throw should do it.

He **flung** the rock right into the crimson-eyed metal skull.

It *pinged* off, not even leaving a dent.

The robot reared up. **"CRIMINAL DAMAGE ATTEMPT DETECTED. LETHAL FORCE AUTHORIZED. NASTY LITTLE HUMAN IS GOING TO GET KEBABBED NOW."**

It shot toward him – and *something swept* down out of the sky, moving too fast to see. It caught U-WOT-M8 in two mechanical claws and lifted the struggling robot up into the air, like a **hawk** making off with a **rabbit.**

Axel watched in awe as it soared overhead: a black-and-green robot with powerful wings, huge talons ... and sad-looking little blue eyes.

"BEAST!" Axel said, with a half laugh

and half sob. "And you went into HARPY form all by yourself! Oh, man, are you a welcome sight right now."

"I ORDER YOU TO LET ME GO!" U-WOT-M8 roared, struggling in BEAST's grip.

"VERY WELL. I OBEY," said BEAST, and dropped it.

"Oh dear," said Axel with relish. "I don't think he really thought that through, did he?"

U-WOT-M8 was too busy plummeting through the air to answer him. The robot bellowed as it fell – not that this made any difference. It waved its arms menacingly, as if it hoped to **scare** the ground into not hitting it. This did not make any difference either.

There was a colossal **SMASH**.

Axel looked down at the smoldering wreckage. An idea occurred to him.

"ARE WE GOING HOME NOW?" BEAST asked.

"Not yet. BEAST, can you scan what's left of that thing's memory?"

"... DO I HAVE TO?" BEAST sounded squeamish.

"If you can. And we need to hurry. Grabbem will be here any moment."

Some time later, BEAST was back in MANTA form, lurking outside the huge underwater door they'd seen earlier.

The Lobstron squatted on a rock nearby, looking grumpier than ever. It hadn't seen them yet.

"Okay. Transmit the codes," said Axel.

BEAST sent the door the security codes he had found in U-WOT-M8's robot brain. The sight of BEAST sticking his fingers into the robot's silver skull, which had still been *fizzling*, had been a grim one. But hopefully it would all have been worthwhile.

The door opened with a slow **rumble.**

The Lobstron came stalking around the corner to see what was going on. Axel drove BEAST into the open door at maximum speed, sending up a cloud of sand, shell and sediment so thick that the Lobstron could barely see at all. **"WHO GOES THERE?"** it croaked.

"IT'S ME, OF COURSE!" yelled Axel, trying to sound as much like U-WOT-M8 as he could.

"FIRST MATE? IS THAT YOU?"

"WHO ELSE WOULD IT BE? GET BACK ON DUTY, **YOU SCAB.**" Axel's throat was getting sore from TALKING LIKE THIS.

"YES, SIR," squeaked the Lobstron. **"SORRY, SIR. DIDN'T SEE IT WAS YOU, SIR."**

"I CAN SMELL YOUR FEAR," Axel added menacingly.

The door slid shut again, to the Lobstron's great relief.

Axel and BEAST were now in a water-filled tunnel so wide you couldn't see the sides. They followed it until it opened into an even wider cavern. Something gigantic was partly submerged in the water ahead of them. A great grayish shape like a **sea monster** – but it was human made. At its front end were massive toothed wheels like **circular-saw** blades.

"There it is," Axel said. "The Plunderer. BEAST, look at the size of that thing. Think what it could do to a coral reef."

"THERE WOULD BE NOTHING LEFT."

Plunderer, thought Axel. *At least they were honest when they named the thing. How are we supposed to stop them now?*

CHAPTER 8

"We need a closer look," Axel said. "The Plunderer is scary, but it still needs the **atomic bomb** or it won't work. And we need to figure out why."

He steered BEAST closer to the Plunderer. BEAST's smart-glass canopy picked out features on the craft: caterpillar tracks, rotary gougers, rock drill, geothermal probe. He frowned.

"What's a geothermal probe?"

"A DEVICE FOR CONVERTING HEAT FROM **MAGMA** INTO ENERGY."

"So it uses magma to charge its batteries. I see. But what's that got to do with an atomic bomb?"

"BEAST DOES NOT KNOW. SORRY. **BEAST IS USELESS AGAIN.**"

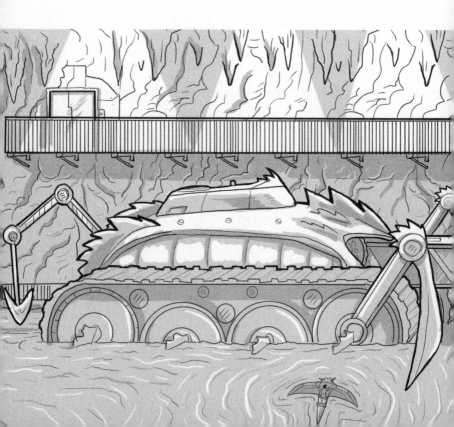

"Stop saying that, BEAST! You're great. Let's see if we can get inside."

Axel brought BEAST up to the water's surface, alongside a jetty.

They were in a cavern like something out of a James Bond film. The top half of the Plunderer took up most of it. The rest was filled with walkways, consoles, cranes, equipment,

pipelines and stacks of supply crates.

Axel couldn't see any guards. He guessed they were all up above, meeting Gus Grabbem Senior now that he'd arrived at the island.

The Plunderer was almost completely submerged, but he could see a sort of turret in the top, with an opening in it. He would be able to fit through, but BEAST wouldn't.

"BEAST, can you wait for me underwater? Stay cloaked. I don't want anyone seeing you."

"PLEASE DO NOT GO INTO THE PLUNDERER, AXEL."

"I've got to!"

"I SENSE GREAT DANGER."

"I promise I'll be careful." Axel looked across at the jetty a few feet away, and pressed the canopy in BEAST's chest, trying to open it. It was **stuck**. Again.

"Arrr!" he yelled. **"What's with this thing? Every time I try to climb out of you, the canopy gets ... stuck ..."**

He stopped.

He seemed to hear his own voice inside his head, explaining things to him in a calm, detached manner: *It's funny, isn't it, how the canopy only ever gets stuck when you're trying to leave BEAST? When you're climbing back into his cockpit, it always opens the first time. It's as if he was trying to keep you from leaving him.*

"BEAST," he said slowly, "I need to talk to you."

"WE CAN TALK LATER, AXEL." BEAST sounded nervous.

"I don't think so." Axel was seriously **angry** now.

"There's nothing wrong with your canopy lock at all, is there? You've been keeping it shut on purpose. You've been trying to keep me **locked in!**"

BEAST said nothing.

"Answer me. It's true, isn't it?"

"**... yes,**" said BEAST, in a very small voice indeed.

"But why?" Axel shouted. "We're meant to be a team. That means being honest with each other!"

"I WAS SCARED YOU WOULD LEAVE ME!" BEAST bawled so loudly it hurt Axel's ears. "YOU KEEP NEEDING TO GO AND DO THINGS THAT BEAST CANNOT DO WITH YOU. ONE DAY YOU WILL GROW UP AND **LEAVE** AND BEAST WILL NEVER SEE YOU AGAIN. BEAST CANNOT BLAME YOU. BEAST IS JUST

SLOWING YOU DOWN."

"**Whoa. Whoa. Steady.** Slowing me down? But … why would you ever think that?"

"WHEN WE WERE TRAINING IN THE JUNKYARD, YOU ONLY WON BECAUSE YOU CLIMBED OUT OF ME," said BEAST gloomily. "AND NOW YOU HAVE YOUR SMART VISOR AND YOU CAN SEE AND YOU DO NOT EVEN NEED BEAST'S HELP WITH THAT ANYMORE. YOU ARE YOUNG AND AGILE AND CLEVER AND BEAST IS **BIG AND CLUMSY AND NOT CLEVER.**"

"We don't have time for this. Let me out, now."

The canopy opened. Axel scrambled onto the jetty and ran toward the Plunderer, not even looking back. BEAST had **lied** to him.

That hurt, but right now he had a mission to focus on.

"Hold it right there, kid!" yelled a voice.

Axel froze.

Scrambling toward him were two figures in guard uniforms. "You aren't meant to be here!" yelled the nearest. "Everyone's supposed to be up top, welcoming Mister Grabbem!"

"Everyone except us," said the second figure, punching the first in the arm. "We got demoted down to full-time guard duty because *someone* kept blowing all our pilot missions."

"Yeah, and that *someone* was you!"

Axel only just managed to keep from **face palming** on the spot.

Of all the people Grabbem could have left to guard the Plunderer, they had to pick these two: Alpha One and Alpha Gold!

Axel had crossed paths with the two

Alpha boys before. They were as mean as rattlesnakes, as treacherous as cobras, and about **as smart as gummy worms.** This was the closest he'd ever been to them, though. Most times they had been chasing him in some kind of vehicle, while he'd been in BEAST. Seeing them in the flesh like this was a shock. One was pale and scrawny, with beady, scowling little eyes, **like a shaved weasel with a moustache.** The other was hefty and grumpy.

"Who are you?" demanded Alpha One.

"What are you doing here?" demanded Alpha Gold.

"Answer my question first," Alpha One said.

Alpha Gold stepped forward. "Don't pay any attention to him. You're **my** prisoner. I saw you first. Answer **my** question."

"No **way** you saw him first!"

Axel kept his mouth tightly shut, thinking: *How am I going to get out of this one?*

While the Alpha boys yelled at one another about whose prisoner Axel was, he quickly **darted** away and ran toward the water. If BEAST was still waiting for him under the surface, he might be able to escape.

"No you don't," hollered Alpha One, and dashed after him. He caught Axel around the waist and **slammed** him to the ground.

"Come on, kid," sneered Alpha Gold. "Where did you think you'd run to?"

"Let's take him up to the mansion," Alpha One said. "Reckon the boss is going to want to have words with him."

"Now that's the first sensible thing you've said all day!"

Axel struggled, but the two Alpha boys were already dragging him toward the elevator. They wrestled him inside. The double doors hissed shut and the elevator began to climb.

Axel thought: *Uh-oh. No way back to BEAST now!*

CHAPTER 9

The elevator trundled upward in awkward silence.

"Still not talking, huh?" said Alpha One.

"You boys don't seem worth talking to," said Axel.

Alpha One frowned at him. "You seem kind of familiar. Have we ever run into you before?"

"Oh, I'm sure I'd remember coming across a pair of guards as tough as you. I think it would stick in my mind forever."

The elevator doors opened.

"This way, **smart mouth,**" grunted Alpha Gold.

"Where are we going to keep him?" mused Alpha One. "This place doesn't have any holding cells."

"I know just the place," said Alpha Gold with a smirk. **"Little bitty storeroom with a keypad lock.** He couldn't guess the combination, not in a million years!"

It took Axel a lot of effort to keep the smile off his face.

The Alpha boys frog-marched him down empty corridors until they reached the storeroom. It was piled high with cleaning products. They pushed Axel in and

slammed the door.

"Listen," said Alpha One. Thumping music was coming from above. "The Grabbems are having a party."

"Let's go join them!" crowed Alpha Gold. "We caught an intruder. We're bound to get **huge promotions** now!"

Axel waited until the sound of their footsteps had died away completely.

Time to go to work, he thought. He adjusted his smart visor and looked at the keypad until the combination popped up. A few quick key presses, and the door lock **clicked open.**

He ran out into the main corridor. There was nobody around.

"Now what?" he whispered to himself. "Find the bomb, and stop it going off. Okay. But where is it?"

He knuckled his forehead in frustration.

Things still didn't add up. Omega had thought the **atomic bomb** had something to do with powering the Plunderer, but now Axel knew the Plunderer used **magma** as a power source. There was no way for both things to be true. Nothing made **sense.** There wasn't even any magma anywhere nearby for it to use ...

Axel froze.

Agent Omega had mentioned an atoll near the island.

What was an atoll?

The remains of a **volcano.**

And what's inside a volcano?

Magma.

The Grabbems were planning to blow up the atoll and restart the volcano, so they could use it as a power source for the Plunderer. *That* was what the bomb was for! They'd have their own **magma** supply. Free energy for the machine that would chew up the ocean floor for hundreds of miles all around!

Axel had to keep moving or he'd be discovered for sure. He found the elevator and thumbed the top button, which was marked **Executive Suites**.

The elevator doors opened onto luxurious corridors carpeted in red, and decked out with chandeliers and golden ornaments. As he tried to figure out which way to go, a guard turned the corner and came right toward him. Axel shoved open the nearest door and dived inside.

The smell hit him first: **sweaty** socks, **old** pizza crusts and **unwashed** underpants. Then the sound: a long, **snotty rattle**. It was a snore.

Axel looked around the room in **awe and**

horror. It must have been a lovely room once. Now, posters covered every part of the walls, showing thrash metal bands covered in face makeup and fake blood. The floor was ankle deep in pizza boxes and crumpled comics. One of the walls was taken up with an enormous TV, under which lay at least five different game consoles and an assortment of games.

In the double bed was a humped figure. That was where the **snoring** – and much of the **smell** – was coming from.

It was Gus Grabbem Junior, Axel's archenemy. Of all the places he could have chosen to hide, he'd picked Gus's personal room.

There was a knock on the door. "Gussie? Sweetums? Are you coming out anytime soon?"

That must be his mom, Axel thought.

The knock came again, louder. "Honey, it's nearly time! We're going to take the yacht over to the atoll, have some lunch, then you get to push **the big red button!**"

Gus mumbled something and stirred.

Axel had to do something, and fast.

He tried to do an imitation of Gus's drawl. "I'm not feeling too good, Mom," he croaked, and added a cough for effect.

"Oh, darling, you sound **_terrible_**! I told you not to eat all that caviar. I'm coming in."

"No!" gasped Axel. "Just let me rest awhile … I'll be fine. I'll be up soon."

"Well, we all can't wait to see you," purred Gus's mother. "Oh, your dad says you and he could maybe go scuba diving and shoot a few fish for the barbecue before **the big kaboom.** But I'll tell him to wait until your tummy settles down."

As Gus's mother moved away, the stirrings of a desperate idea took shape in Axel's mind. It meant digging through the **disgusting junk** that lay all around this room, but he'd just have to hold his nose and hope his stomach could stand it.

He rummaged around until he found Gus's scuba outfit. While Gus snored, he quickly changed into it. The tight material covered his entire body, except for his face. He used some athlete's foot powder to make his skin look paler, pulled the diving mask on and hoped that would be enough to disguise him.

"Should work, if nobody looks too closely," he muttered. "The things I have to do to **save the world!**"

Crossing his fingers, he headed out and took the elevator down to the ground floor of the mansion.

The hallway was crowded with Grabbem staff. Guards stood on every corner. Nobody stopped him as he walked past. Some of them even saluted.

His heartbeat thumped in his ears. *They all think I'm Gus. So far, so good.* He felt very exposed without BEAST's comforting, armored body covering him.

He continued down the path and out over the sandy beach.

The Grabbem yacht was moored just off the shore. On the deck, **Gus Grabbem Senior** and his wife were lounging in deck chairs, wearing sunglasses, looking out over the sea as if they were about to enjoy a pleasure cruise. Captain Fenton loomed over them.

"Gussie! Take a seat. Nearly time for **the big *kaboom!*"** called Gus Grabbem Senior.

He waved a handheld device. There was a big red button on it.

"You should be grateful. Your dad spent a lot of money on this **atom bomb,**" said Captain Fenton.

"And we've only got the one," added Gus Grabbem Senior. "So let's make the most of it, eh?"

Axel glanced nervously at the sea's surface. There was no sign of BEAST.

The next moment a shout rang out from the mansion. "Mom? Dad? Where's my scuba gear?"

Axel spun around to see a very angry Gus Grabbem Junior striding down the beach. He saw Axel and his eyes grew wide. "What – **who are you?**"

"We thought that was you, Gussie!" his mother frowned.

"Of course it's not me, you dozy old bat! *I'm* me. That guy there is an **impostor**, and he's wearing my stuff!" Gus was practically hopping on the spot with rage.

Gus Grabbem Senior stood up, casting a broad, threatening shadow over the water. "Guards, **get him!**"

CHAPTER 10

Six or seven guards immediately charged down from the house, running right at Axel.

Gus Grabbem Junior came running at him, too. **"Get that mask off,"** he yelled. "I want a good look at you!"

With the Grabbems and their guards closing in, Axel had only one move left.

He sprinted down toward the beach and waded into the water.

"Don't worry, son!" bellowed Gus Grabbem Senior. "I'll get the little **blighter** for you!" He ran to the railing and dived over the edge, still holding the big red button.

But the splash never came. A metal tentacle shot up from the water and caught Gus Grabbem Senior around the ankle. He dangled in the air, **howling** and **flailing** his arms around.

Axel saw two familiar-looking blue eyes shining dimly under the water. It was BEAST – and he was in OCTO form!

"BEAST! Good to see you. We need to stop that bomb!"

BEAST shook Gus Grabbem Senior like a bottle of ketchup. The big red button fell out of his hands. BEAST caught it deftly with another tentacle and **flung** it far out to sea.

"Nooooo!" screamed Gus Grabbem

Junior. **"My bomb!"**

BEAST struck out with two more of his tentacles, knocking the oncoming Grabbem guards off their feet. They **floundered** in the shallows.

He dropped Gus Grabbem Senior into the water, then picked up Axel, gently lowered him into his cockpit, and sealed the canopy. They dived back under the surface.

"Get us to the atoll," Axel gasped. "The moment they find that big red button, the bomb's going to go off!"

They went powering through the water as fast as BEAST could travel.

"AXEL?" said BEAST. "I AM SORRY."

"Me, too. Let's never fight like that again, okay?"

"OKAY."

They **roared** along just under the surface.

The atoll appeared on the horizon.

The next moment, a torpedo shot past them and exploded. Axel checked behind them. Three mini-submarines were in pursuit, and the one in the front was a shiny black model bristling with weapons.

"Gus and the Alpha boys," he said. "I knew they wouldn't let us go that easily."

BEAST spun around in the water. He raised all eight of his metal tentacles. Another torpedo came **whizzing** toward them, but BEAST struck out with a tentacle like a whiplash and knocked it off course.

Gus Grabbem Junior's voice came hissing over the radio. "I should have figured it was you, **donkey boy!** How does my scuba gear feel, huh? Just can't resist stealing my stuff, can you?"

"Those subs are powerful," Axel said.

"One hit and we're finished."

"WE CAN FIGHT THEM, AXEL," BEAST said bravely. "TOGETHER."

"But it's three against one!"

"THREE AGAINST **TWO.**"

The subs closed in. Axel gripped the controls and got ready to fight. If a **battle royal** was what Gus wanted, they'd give him one …

"No!" he heard himself saying. "No, this is wrong. We don't need to fight. We need to get rid of that bomb!"

"AXEL?"

"BEAST, get out of the water. Shift to HARPY form. Hurry!"

Inside his lethal mini-sub, Gus Grabbem Junior licked his lips and grinned in anticipation. The boy who'd stolen his robot had gotten away too many times. Now, at last, they could settle this.

Then he saw that BEAST had turned around again and was speeding toward the surface.

"Chicken!" he screeched. "I see you, running away! What's wrong? Don't have the guts to fight? Well, I win this one! I win and you lose! **YOU LOSE!**"

The words stung Axel's pride, but he forced himself to ignore them. They could have a rematch another time. He had bigger fish to fry right now.

BEAST shifted form as he broke the water's surface. His arms expanded out into wide metal wings. His feet sprouted long claws. He looked like a winged dinosaur, or a harpy out of the ancient myths.

"There's the atoll," Axel said. "And I see the bomb. BEAST, use your claws. Try to grab it."

BEAST swooped in toward the silver cylinder that lay in the atoll's lagoon. His claws caught hold of it. Then they were rising back up through the air, hauling the deadly cargo with them.

"WHERE SHALL I PUT IT?" BEAST asked.

Axel thought quickly. "Where's the safest place on Earth to detonate an **atomic bomb?**"

"PERHAPS THE MIDDLE OF THE NEVADA DESERT, BUT WE CANNOT REACH THERE IN TIME."

"Oh, man. **Talk about a hot potato.** I need to come up with an idea, and fast!"

"I AM SORRY, AXEL. CREATURES WILL BE AT RISK WHEREVER IT IS DETONATED. THERE IS NO TRULY SAFE

PLACE ON EARTH TO EXPLODE SUCH A BOMB."

Axel's mouth fell open. "No safe place **on Earth**. Of course. That's the answer."

"EXPLAIN?"

"BEAST, keep flying up. Fly as high as you can."

"AND THEN?"

"Then just keep going."

So BEAST, trusting Axel completely, did as he was told.

He flew up until the islands below were tiny green flecks in a mantle of blue. He flew up past the clouds, up to where the air was freezing and thin. Soon his wings began to groan and his body **shook** from the strain.

"I CANNOT CLIMB ANY HIGHER IN THIS FORM, AXEL. I WILL BE DESTROYED."

"Change form. **Shift to ORBITA.**"

BEAST began to transform. Solar panels unfolded from his back. The arm-wings vanished, to be replaced with complicated grabbers. Little rockets emerged from his thighs. Axel saw new readouts appearing, showing oxygen levels and orbital speed.

The rockets fired. BEAST shot straight up again, heading away from Earth. Axel held his breath as the horizon steadily became more and more curved. He could make out whole continents now.

"INCOMING SIGNAL. DEVICE IS ABOUT TO **DETONATE**," warned BEAST.

"Looks like they found the big red button. Quick, let's get rid of it!"

BEAST hurled the bomb away from them. It **spun** silently away into space, far away from any living creature that it could harm.

KA-BOOOOOOOM!

For an instant, space lit up with the brightness of a second sun. Axel shielded his eyes. The **atomic blast** expanded out in a brilliant, colorful aurora, not the mushroom cloud Axel had expected. For something so deadly, it was strangely beautiful.

As he watched, the **firestorm** slowly died away and the peaceful darkness of space closed in once again. Axel felt peaceful, too. The fearsome bomb hadn't harmed even a barnacle.

"There it goes. We did it. It's over."

"WE DID IT," echoed BEAST.

"No bomb, no volcano. No geothermal power source. The Plunderer's useless to them now."

"BEAST FELT USELESS, TOO. BUT NOT ANYMORE."

"Good. Because you're not. You're amazing. And you're my **best friend.**"

"SHALL WE GO HOME?"

"Not just yet. We're in space! I want to make the most of it."

Now he could relax and enjoy the view. Axel looked out over the bright field of stars and the darkness between them, deeper even than the blackness far beneath the sea.

He felt very small, but not in a way that made him feel scared. He knew the stars were many light years away, but he felt closer to them than ever. The universe was **unthinkably big,** but he and BEAST still had a place in it, and they belonged there.

He turned to look at Earth, hanging beside them in space.

That's the place BEAST and I are sworn to protect, he thought. *I've never seen her like this before. It feels like saying "hello" face-to-face, for the first time.*

He watched the planet in silence for a few moments, thinking how **lucky** he was. If it hadn't been for BEAST, he never would have had this experience.

"You know, BEAST," he said, "this new smart visor is great, and it means I can do more by myself. But that doesn't mean I need you any less."

"REALLY?"

"Really! I nearly got myself killed back there – more than once! You came through for me, though. I know I can count on you."

BEAST thought about that. "PERHAPS AXEL IS NOT GOING TO OUTGROW BEAST ANYTIME SOON. PERHAPS BEAST HAS BEEN WORRYING FOR **NO REASON.**"

"Don't sweat it, big guy. It happens to us all now and then." Axel grinned. "Come on. Let's go home."